Geronimo Stilton
ENGLISH!

8 AROUND THE WORLD 環遊世界

新雅文化事業有限公司
www.sunya.com.hk

Geronimo Stilton English
AROUND THE WORLD 環遊世界

作　　者：Geronimo Stilton 謝利連摩·史提頓
譯　　者：申倩
責任編輯：王燕參
封面繪圖：Giuseppe Facciotto
插圖繪畫：Claudio Cernuschi, Andrea Denegri, Daria Cerchi
內文設計：Angela Ficarelli, Raffaella Picozzi
出　　版：新雅文化事業有限公司
　　　　　香港筲箕灣耀興道3號東匯廣場9樓
　　　　　營銷部電話：（852）2562 0161
　　　　　客戶服務部電話：（852）2976 6559
　　　　　傳真：（852）2597 4003
　　　　　網址：http://www.sunya.com.hk
　　　　　電郵：marketing@sunya.com.hk
發　　行：香港聯合書刊物流有限公司
　　　　　香港新界大埔汀麗路36號中華商務印刷大廈3字樓
　　　　　電話：（852）2150 2100　傳真：（852）2407 3062
　　　　　電郵：info@suplogistics.com.hk
印　　刷：C & C Offset Printing Co.,Ltd
　　　　　香港新界大埔汀麗路36號
版　　次：二〇一一年二月初版
　　　　　10 9 8 7 6 5 4 3 2 1

CONTENTS
目錄

BENJAMIN'S CLASSMATES
班哲文的老師和同學們

Maestra Topitilla
托比蒂拉・德・托比莉斯

Rarin
拉琳

Diego
迪哥

Rupa
露芭

Tui
杜爾

David
大衛

Sakura
櫻花

Mohamed
穆哈麥德

Tian Kai
田凱

Oliver
奧利佛

Milenko
米蘭哥

Trippo
特里普

Carmen
卡敏

Atina
阿提娜

Esmeralda
愛絲梅拉達

Pandora
潘朵拉

Takeshi
北野

Kuti
菊花

Benjamin
班哲文

Hsing
阿星

Laura
羅拉

Kiku
奇哥

Antonia
安東妮婭

Liza
麗莎

GERONIMO AND HIS FRIENDS

謝利連摩和他的家鼠朋友們

謝利連摩‧史提頓 Geronimo Stilton
一個古怪的傢伙，簡直可以說是一隻笨拙的文化鼠。他是《鼠民公報》的總裁，正花盡心思改變報紙業的歷史。

菲‧史提頓 Tea Stilton
謝利連摩的妹妹，她是《鼠民公報》的特派記者，同時也是一個運動愛好者。

班哲文‧史提頓 Benjamin Stilton
謝利連摩的小侄兒，常被叔叔稱作「我的小乳酪」，是一隻感情豐富的小老鼠。

潘朵拉‧華之鼠 Pandora Woz
柏蒂‧活力鼠的小侄女、班哲文最好的朋友，是一隻活潑開朗的小老鼠。

柏蒂‧活力鼠 Patty Spring
美麗迷人的電視新聞工作者，致力於她熱愛的電視事業。

賴皮 Trappola
謝利連摩的表弟，非常喜歡食物，風趣幽默，是一隻饞嘴、愛開玩笑的老鼠，善於將歡樂傳遞給每一隻鼠。

麗萍姑媽 Zia Lippa
謝利連摩的姑媽，對鼠十分友善，又和藹可親，只想將最好的給身邊的鼠。

艾拿 Iena
謝利連摩的好朋友，充滿活力，熱愛各項運動，他希望能把對運動的熱誠傳給謝利連摩。

史奎克‧愛管閒事鼠 Ficcanaso Squitt
謝利連摩的好朋友，是一個非常有頭腦的私家偵探，總是穿着一件黃色的乾濕樓。

GEOGRAPHY LESSON
上地理課

親愛的小朋友，我們正準備開始一段與別不同的環遊世界之旅了！你不相信自己的耳朵？！是的，我知道，你們都很了解我：我不喜歡旅行，儘管我的朋友們總是令我經歷一次又一次旅行⋯⋯但這次我卻是迫不及待想出發，你知道為什麼嗎？因為這次是跟托比蒂拉老師、班哲文和潘朵拉，以及他們的同學們一起利用地球儀去環遊世界啊！

Stay with us Mr. Stilton, the kids will be happy.

Yeees!

What lesson have you got today?
你們今天上什麼課呀？
to start with
以……開始

跟我謝利連摩·史提頓一起學英文，就像玩遊戲一樣簡單好玩！

你可以一邊看着圖畫一邊讀。
以下有幾個標誌，你要特別留意：

當看到 標誌時，你可以聽CD，一邊聽，一邊跟着朗讀，還可以跟着一起唱歌。

當看到 ★ 標誌時，你可以和朋友們一起玩遊戲，或者嘗試回答問題。題目很簡單，它們對鞏固你所學過的內容很有幫助。

當看到 ❗ 標誌時，你要注意看一下格子裏的生字，反覆唸幾遍，掌握發音。

最後，不要忘記完成小測驗和練習冊裏的問題！看看你有多聰明吧。

祝大家學得開開心心！

謝利連摩·史提頓

THE GLOBE 地球儀

托比蒂拉老師開始向學生們介紹地球和它的七大洲：可以從北遊到南，從東遊到西！請你用英語跟着讀吧！

North Pole	北極	east	東方
Arctic regions	北極地區	south	南方
South Pole	南極	west	西方
Antarctic regions	南極地區	hemisphere	半球
equator	赤道	northern hemisphere	北半球
north	北方	southern hemisphere	南半球

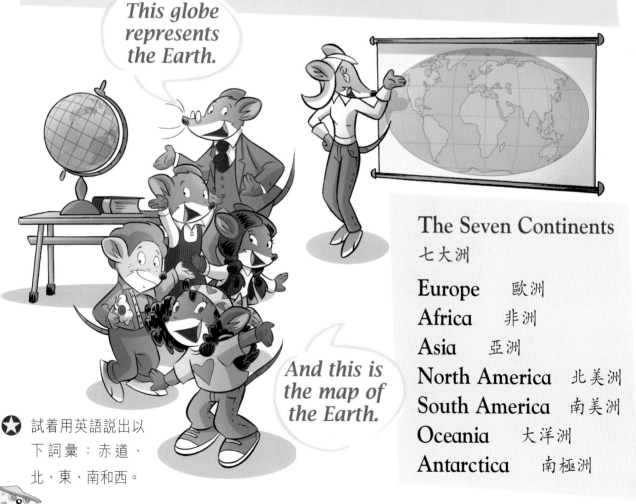

This globe represents the Earth.

And this is the map of the Earth.

The Seven Continents
七大洲

Europe	歐洲
Africa	非洲
Asia	亞洲
North America	北美洲
South America	南美洲
Oceania	大洋洲
Antarctica	南極洲

⭐ 試着用英語説出以下詞彙：赤道、北、東、南和西。

答案：equator, north, east, south and west.

It's very hot near the equator. It only rains during the rainy season.

The Arctic and Antarctic regions around the North Pole and the South Pole are the coldest.

Natural Habitats
自然棲息地

desert　沙漠

savannah　熱帶稀樹草原

tropical rainforest　熱帶雨林

coniferous forest　針葉林

temperate forest　溫帶樹林

tundra　凍土層

Mediterranean scrub
地中海灌木叢

grassland　草原

polar regions　極地地區

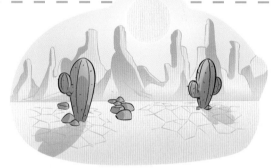

It's very hot during the day and very cold at night in the desert.

When it's winter in the northern hemisphere, it's summer in the southern hemisphere.

9

TIME ZONES 時區

　　到世界各地旅遊時，需要調校好你的手錶。地球分為24個時區，每個時區內的國家都使用同一個時間，而當你去到另一個時區的國家時，時間便會隨之改變。時區的標準起點是英國格林威治：當你從這裏出發向東走，每到一個時區就需要加一小時，如果你向西走，則每到一個時區就減一小時。跟着我算一算，現在在羅馬、紐約和北京分別是幾點鐘？

Let's look at the time zones!

North

West

New York

San Francisco

To go from Hong Kong, in China, to New York, in the United States of America, you have to go west and there are twelve time zones less. When it's 7 p.m. in Hong Kong, it's 7 a.m. in New York.

To go from London, in Great Britain, to Beijing, in China, you have to go east and there are eight time zones more. When it's 8 a.m. in London, it's 4 p.m. in Beijing.

Let's see what time it is in different cities at the same moment.

To go from Rome, in Italy, to San Francisco, in the United States of America, you have to go west and there are nine time zones less. When it's 9 a.m. in Rome, it's midnight in San Francisco.

! look at 看

East

London

Rome

Beijing

Madrid

Hong Kong

New Delhi

South

To go from Madrid, in Spain, to New Delhi, in India, you have to go east and there are five time zones more. When it's 2 p.m. in Madrid, it's 7 p.m. in New Delhi.

11

NATIONS, LANGUAGES, FLAGS
認識不同的國家、語言和國旗

班哲文的同班同學很多是來自世界各地的，於是托比蒂拉老師請他們作自我介紹，告訴大家他們來自哪個國家和哪個大洲，你也跟著一起說說看。

Europe

I come from Italy. I'm Italian. I speak Italian.

Italy is very famous for its monuments.

I come from Germany. I'm German. I speak German.

Berlin is the capital of Germany.

I come from Greece. I'm Greek. I speak Greek.

I love Greek history.

I come from Spain. I'm Spanish. I speak Spanish.

Lots of people dance the flamenco in Spain.

Africa

I come from Morocco. I'm Moroccan. I speak Arabic.

In Morocco, there's the Sahara Desert.

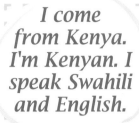

I come from Kenya. I'm Kenyan. I speak Swahili and English.

There are lots of wildlife parks in Kenya.

! everybody　每個人

Everybody loves carnival.　每個人都喜歡狂歡節。

America

I come from the United States of America. I'm American. I speak English.

American people love baseball.

I come from Brazil. I'm Brazilian. I speak Portuguese.

Everybody loves carnival in Brazil.

I'm Chinese.
我是中國人。

Italian
意大利人 / 意大利語
German
德國人 / 德語
Greek
希臘人 / 希臘語
Spanish
西班牙人 / 西班牙語
Moroccan　摩洛哥人
Kenyan　肯雅人
American　美國人
Brazilian　巴西人
Chinese　中國人
Mandarin　國語
Japanese　日本人 / 日語
Malay　馬來人 / 馬來語
Australian　澳洲人

14

Oceania

I have a friend in Australia. He is Australian. He speaks English.

There are kangaroos in Australia.

A Coloured World

A SONG FOR YOU! Track 1

Italy, Brazil, Greece, Japan…
I'm Japanese, I speak Japanese!
Switzerland, France, Spain, England…
I'm English, I speak English!
Germany, Ireland, Portugal, Spain…
I'm Spanish, I speak Spanish!
But now we speak English, all together!
But now we speak English, all together!

Albania, Russia, India, China…
I'm Chinese, I speak Chinese!
Canada, Ecuador, Iraq, Cuba…
I'm Cuban, I speak Spanish!
Kenya, Scotland, Mexico, Peru…
I'm Peruvian, I speak Spanish, too!
But now we speak English, all together!
But now we speak English, all together!

DEAR FRIENDS...
親愛的朋友們……

班哲文、潘朵拉和他們的同學請我多待一會兒，他們向我讀出由世界各地的朋友寄來的信。你也跟着他們一起讀出來吧！

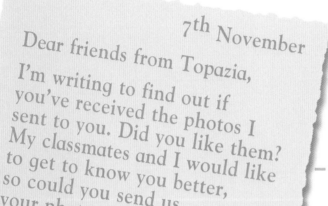

7th November

Dear friends from Topazia,

I'm writing to find out if you've received the photos I sent to you. Did you like them? My classmates and I would like to get to know you better, so could you send us your photos, too?

Bye,
your friend Guo from China

We would like to get to know you better.

我們想知道更多關於你的事情。

8th July

Dear Rarin,

How are you? And how about your friends? I'm fine and very happy because I'm spending my summer holidays at the seaside. What about you? Write to me and tell me about your holidays.

Love,
Yannis from Greece

What about you?
你呢？

讀完了朋友們的來信後，現在輪到讀出班哲文和潘朵拉他們寫給朋友們的回信了。你也跟着一起大聲讀出來吧！

30th May

Dear Andres,

Thanks for your letter and the drawing you sent me, it's so colourful and beautiful! Our teacher Topitilla hung it on the door of our classroom, so we can see it every day. I love taking pictures instead, and I'm sending you a picture of a flower: do you like it? Answer soon!

Your friend,
Pandora from Topazia

Thanks for your letter!
謝謝你寫信給我！
Answer soon!
希望很快就能收到你的回信！

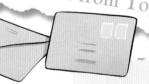

3rd November

Dear Olia,

What's the weather like in your country in November? In my town it's cold and foggy. I like to stay home, cosy and warm, reading, drawing and playing with friends. How about you? How do you spend your free time in this season? I'm curious and would like to know. Please write soon.

Love,
Benjamin from Topazia

7th November
11月7日

17

THE TRAIN OF FRIENDSHIP
友誼號火車

托比蒂拉老師邀請我和大家一起唱一首他們班自己編寫的歌曲，這是一首關於友誼的歌，你也跟着一起唱吧！

The Train of Friendship

A SONG FOR YOU! Track 2

The train of friendship.
The train of friendship.
There's a train crossing the mountains,
the plains, the deserts, the cities of the world.
It is the train of friendship
full of children like me, like you!

If you travel all over the world,
you'll find many friends,
it doesn't matter what colour your skin is,
if you're looking for friendship!
The train of friendship.
The train of friendship.
It's nice to have many friends
in every corner of the world!
It is nice to know that someone beyond the sea
is thinking of you, yes, of you!

If you travel all over the world,
you'll find many friends,
it doesn't matter what colour your skin is,
if you're looking for friendship!
The train of friendship.
The train of friendship.

唱完歌後，托比蒂拉老師還跟大家玩一個遊戲，讓大家在歡樂的氣氛中結束一天的學習！請你跟着托比蒂拉老師學習說出遊戲的規則，這樣你就可以向你的朋友介紹這個有趣的遊戲，並且和他們一起玩了！

How to Play

❶ Everybody, except for Benjamin, takes a cushion and puts it on the floor, in a circle.

❷ While the music is playing, Benjamin, Pandora and their friends dance around the cushions.

❸ When the music stops, everyone tries to sit on a cushion.

❹ The one left without a cushion is out and takes another cushion away.

❺ The game is over when there's only one player left and no cushions!

everyone
每個人
Everyone tries to sit on a cushion.
每個人都嘗試找一個靠墊坐下來。

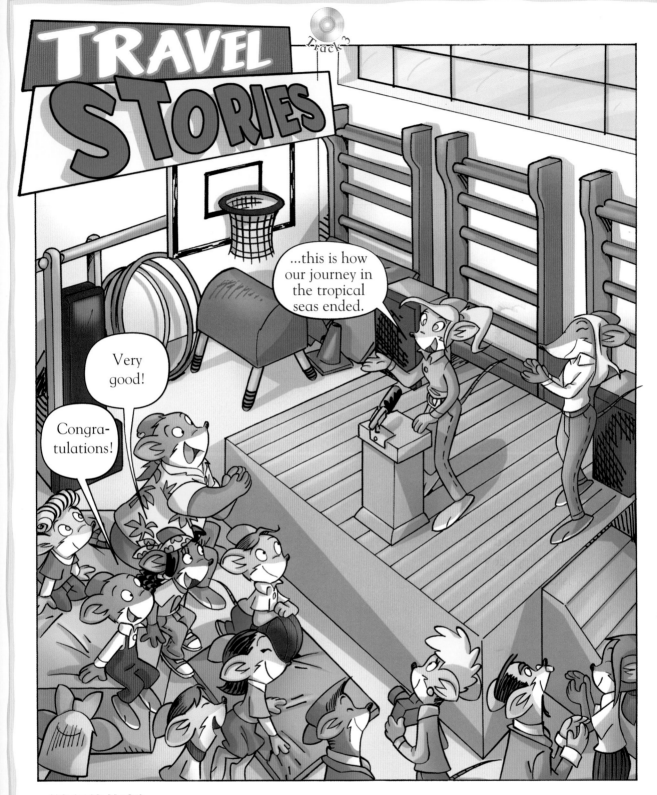

〈旅行的故事〉

柏蒂：……我們的熱帶海上之旅就這樣結束了。

潘朵拉：好極了！

班哲文：恭喜你！

Thanks for your speech on 'travelling'.

Thank you! You've organized a fantastic end-of-the-year school party!

托比蒂拉：謝謝你給大家分享你的旅遊見聞。

柏蒂：不用客氣。你為學校籌備了一個別出心裁的結業禮呢。

Thank you! I wanted to tell you about the day I left for the Topucche Island...

賴皮：多謝！我想講給大家聽，自從我離開老鼠島那日起⋯⋯

Now, let's listen to another travel story...

...by our Benjamin Stilton's uncle!

托比蒂拉：現在，讓我們一起來聽另一個關於旅行的故事，為我們演講的是班哲文・史提頓的叔叔！

Uhm...I have the honor of presenting Geronimo Stilton!

Great!

Uhm...

托比蒂拉：唔⋯⋯很榮幸為大家介紹謝利連摩・史提頓先生！

觀眾們：太好了！

賴皮：哦⋯⋯

21

Do we travel to relax, to visit faraway places, to keep fit or to have new experiences?

謝利連摩：我們去旅行是想放鬆一下，想去一些較遠的地方看看，想健身，還是想得到一些新的體驗？

Trappola's answer is: to relax!

賴皮的答案是：想放鬆一下。

I say: it depends...

Once, I spent a week in the mountains trying to relax. The sun was shining and the air was chilly...

對我來說，這要視乎情況……
有一次，我到山上去待了一個星期，想放鬆一下。太陽高高的照耀着，但空氣仍有點冷……

Patty, Benjamin and Pandora went for a walk while I decided to spend my time tasting some local cheese...

柏蒂、班哲文和潘朵拉一起去散步，而我則決定自己留下來品嘗一下當地的乳酪……

在那裏，我第一次嘗到乳酪竟可以這般辣！
我感覺到渾身快要燒着了！

於是我拼命跑……

謝利連摩：啊啊啊啊啊啊！
柏蒂／潘朵拉／班哲文：？！？

The End

……然後我成了第一個到達山頂！
柏蒂：謝利連摩，你到了這裏多久了？
謝利連摩：唔……已有一段時間了……

謝利連摩：所以，當你去旅行時，不必做任何計劃！但如果你真的要計劃，那就注意一下自己的飲食吧！

23

TEST 小測驗

⭐ 1. 把下面的句子和相配的圖畫用線連起來。

(a) It's very hot during the day and very cold at night in the desert. ●

A.  ●

(b) It's very hot near the equator. ●

B.  ●

(c) The Arctic and Antarctic regions are the coldest. ●

C. ●

⭐ 2. 用英語說出下面的國家名稱。

(a) 意大利　　(b) 西班牙　　(c) 希臘　　(d) 德國　　(e) 美國

⭐ 3. 用英語說出下面的句子。

(a) 我是中國人。　　(b) 我是日本人。

(c) 我是肯雅人。　　(d) 我是西班牙人。

(e) 我們是意大利人，我們說意大利語。

(f) 我是德國人，我說德語。

(g) 我們是希臘人，我們說希臘語。

(h) 我是美國人，我說英語。

DICTIONARY 詞典

（英、粵、普發聲）

A

Africa　非洲

Albania　阿爾巴尼亞

Antarctic regions　南極地區

Antarctica　南極洲

Arabic　阿拉伯語

Arctic regions　北極地區

Asia　亞洲

Australia　澳洲

Australian　澳洲人

B

baseball　棒球

Brazil　巴西

Brazilian　巴西人

C

Canada　加拿大

capital　首都

carnival　狂歡節

China　中國

Chinese　中國人

chopsticks　筷子

classmates　同學

classroom　課室

cold　冷

coniferous forest　針葉林

continents　大洲

cosy　舒適的

Cuba　古巴

curious　好奇的

cushion　靠墊

D

day　白天

desert　沙漠

different　不同的

E

east　東方

Ecuador　厄瓜多爾

England　英格蘭

equator　赤道

Europe　歐洲

F

famous　著名的

find out　找出

flamenco　佛蘭明高舞

foggy　多霧的

France　法國

friendship　友誼

G

geography　地理

German　德國人 / 德語

Germany　德國

get to know　想知道

globe　地球儀

grassland　草原

Greece　希臘

Greek　希臘人 / 希臘語

H

habitats　棲息地

hemisphere　半球

history　歷史

holidays　假期

hot　熱

I

India　印度

Iraq　伊拉克

Ireland　愛爾蘭

Italian　意大利人 / 意大利語

Italy　意大利

J

Japan　日本

Japanese　日本人 / 日語

journey　旅程

K

kangaroos　袋鼠

Kenya　肯雅

Kenyan　肯雅人

L

languages　語言

M

Malaysia　馬來西亞

Malay　馬來人 / 馬來語

Mandarin　國語

map　地圖

Mediterranean scrub

　　地中海灌木叢

Mexico　墨西哥

Moroccan　摩洛哥人

Morocco　摩洛哥

monuments　歷史遺跡

mountains　山

N

nations　國家

natural　自然的

night　晚上

north　北方

North America　北美洲

North Pole　北極

northern hemisphere　北半球

O

Oceania　大洋洲

P

Peru　秘魯

Peruvian　秘魯人

photo　照片

plains　平原

polar regions　極地地區

Portugal　葡萄牙

Portuguese

　　葡萄牙人 / 葡萄牙語

R

rains　下雨

rainy season　雨季

Russia　俄羅斯

S

Sahara Desert　撒哈拉沙漠

savannah　熱帶稀樹草原

Scotland　蘇格蘭

seaside　海邊

season　季節

see　看見

south　南方

South America　南美洲

South Pole　南極

southern hemisphere　南半球

Spain　西班牙

Spanish

　西班牙人 / 西班牙語

Switzerland　瑞士

start with　以……開始

stay　留下

story　故事

summer　夏天

Swahili　斯華西里語

T

talk　講

tell　告訴

temperate forest　温帶樹林

tigers　老虎

time zones　時區

travel　旅遊

tropical rainforest　熱帶雨林

tundra　凍土層

U

use　使用

W

walk　散步

west　西方

wildlife parks　野生動物園

winter　冬天

world　世界

看在一千塊莫澤雷勒乳酪的份上，你學得開心嗎？很開心，對不對？好極了！跟你一起跳舞唱歌我也很開心！我等着你下次繼續跟班哲文和潘朵拉一起玩一起學英語呀。現在要說再見了，當然是用英語說啦！

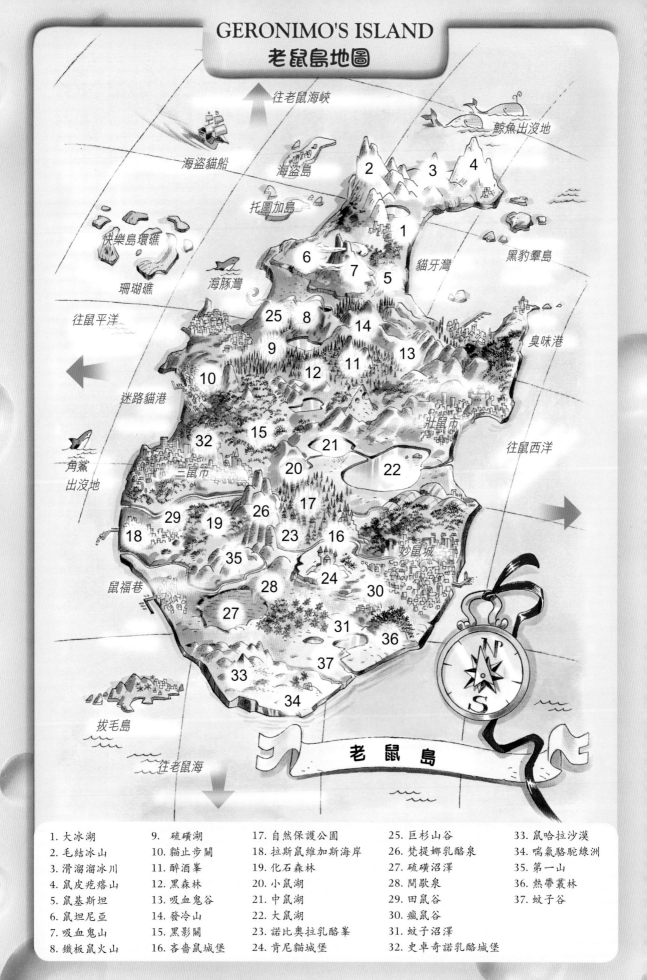

GERONIMO'S ISLAND
老鼠島地圖

往老鼠海峽

鯨魚出沒地

海盜貓船

海盜島

托圖加島

快樂島環礁

珊瑚礁

海豚灣

往鼠平洋

迷路貓港

角鯊
出沒地

鼠福巷

拔毛島

往老鼠海

貓牙灣

黑豹羣島

臭味港

壯鼠市

往鼠西洋

三鼠市

妙鼠城

老 鼠 島

1. 大冰湖
2. 毛結冰山
3. 滑溜溜冰川
4. 鼠皮疙瘩山
5. 鼠基斯坦
6. 鼠坦尼亞
7. 吸血鬼山
8. 鐵板鼠火山

9. 硫磺湖
10. 貓止步關
11. 醉酒峯
12. 黑森林
13. 吸血鬼谷
14. 發冷山
15. 黑影關
16. 客魯鼠城堡

17. 自然保護公園
18. 拉斯鼠維加斯海岸
19. 化石森林
20. 小鼠湖
21. 中鼠湖
22. 大鼠湖
23. 諾比奧拉乳酪峯
24. 肯尼貓城堡

25. 巨杉山谷
26. 梵提娜乳酪泉
27. 硫磺沼澤
28. 間歇泉
29. 田鼠谷
30. 瘋鼠谷
31. 蚊子沼澤
32. 史卓奇諾乳酪城堡

33. 鼠哈拉沙漠
34. 喘氣駱駝綠洲
35. 第一山
36. 熱帶叢林
37. 蚊子谷

Geronimo Stilton

EXERCISE BOOK
練習冊

想知道自己對 AROUND THE WOPLD 掌握了多少，
趕快打開後面的練習完成它吧！

ENGLISH!

8 **AROUND THE WOPLD** 環遊世界

GEOGRAPHY LESSON
上地理課

⭐ 把下面的句子重新排列成有意思的段落，在 ☐ 內裏填寫代表正確答案的英文字母。

A.

> Let's play with the ball globe to start with!

B.

> What lesson have you got today?

> Geography! We're going to talk about the world, Uncle G!

C.

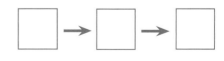

☐ → ☐ → ☐

THE GLOBE 地球儀

★ 從下面選出適當的英文詞彙填在橫線上。

> Earth　　　map　　　globe　　　continents

This
1. _____
represents the
2. _____ .

And this is the
3. _____
of the Earth.

We can
see the seven
4. _____ !

THE MAP 地圖

⭐ 從下面選出適當的英文詞彙填在橫線上。

season	cold	desert	coldest	hot
equator	North Pole	hemisphere	winter	

1. It's very hot near the_____ . It only rains during the rainy_____ .

2. The Arctic and Antarctic regions, around the _____ and the South Pole, are the _____ !

3. It's very_____ during the day and very _____ at night in the_____ .

4. When it's_____ in the northern hemisphere, it's summer in the southern_____ .

NATURAL HABITATS
自然棲息地

⭐ 迪哥和羅拉想在下面的字母迷宮中圈出以下的生字，你可以幫助他們嗎？圈圈看。

desert	grassland	rainforest
savannah	scrub	tundra

n	g	q	r	y	u	c	w
v	r	h	c	v	i	r	r
s	a	v	a	n	n	a	h
s	s	e	m	v	n	i	r
c	s	a	s	b	b	n	r
y	l	o	c	i	w	f	e
o	a	s	r	z	e	o	r
s	n	t	u	n	d	r	a
b	d	w	b	a	e	e	g
r	v	u	k	c	n	s	f
d	d	e	s	e	r	t	l

DEAR FRIENDS 親愛的朋友們

★ 把下列的英文詞彙填在句子中適當的橫線上，或重新排列次序寫在橫線上，使句子的意思變得完整。

1. My classmates and I would _____ to get to

_____ you _____ .

better	like	know

2. I'm spending my summer holidays at the seaside.

_____ ?

about	What	you

3. _____ and I'm sending

you a picture of a flower: do you like it?

love	taking	I	pictures

4. _____

_____ in November?

like	What's	country	weather
in	your	the	

DIFFERENT NATIONS AND LANGUAGES
不同的國家和語言

⭐ 根據圖畫和提示，在橫線上填寫正確的答案。（選項可用多於一次）

Chinese　Mandarin　Malay　Brazilian　Kenyan
Portuguese　Moroccan　Arabic　German
Japanese　Italian　Greek　American　English

1. I come from China. I'm _____ .
   I speak_____ .

2. I come from Morocco. I'm _____ .
   I speak _____ .

3. I come from Italy. I'm _____ .
   I speak _____ .

4. I come from Malaysia. I'm _____ .
   I speak _____ .

5. I come from Germany. I'm _____ .

I speak_____ .

6. I come from Greece. I'm _____ .

I speak_____ .

7. I come from the United States of America. I'm_____ . I speak _____ .

8. I come from Kenya. I'm _____ .

I speak Swahili and _____ .

9. I come from Japan. I'm _____ .

I speak _____ .

10. I come from Brazil. I'm _____ .

I speak _____ .

TEST 小測驗

1. (a) B   2. (b) A   3. (c) C
2. (a) Italy   (b) Spain   (c) Greece   (d) Germany   (e) the United States of America
3. (a) I am Chinese.   (b) I am Japanese.   (c) I am Kenyan.   (d) I am Spanish.
   (e) We are Italian, we speak Italian.   (f) I am German, I speak German.
   (g) We are Greek, we speak Greek.   (h) I am American, I speak English.

EXERCISE BOOK 練習冊

P.1
B→C→A

P.2
1. globe   2. Earth   3. map   4. continents

P.3
1. equator, season   2. North Pole, coldest   3. hot, cold, desert   4. winter, hemisphere

P.4

n	g	q	r	y	u	c	w
v	r	h	c	v	i	r	r
s	a	v	a	n	n	a	h
s	s	e	m	v	n	i	r
c	s	a	s	b	b	n	r
y	l	o	c	i	w	f	e
o	a	s	r	z	e	o	r
s	n	t	u	n	d	r	a
b	d	w	b	a	e	e	g
r	v	u	k	c	n	s	f
d	d	e	s	e	r	t	l

P.5
1. My classmates and I would <u>like</u> to get to <u>know</u> you <u>better</u>.
2. I'm spending my summer holidays at the seaside. <u>What about you</u>?
3. <u>I love taking pictures</u> and I'm sending you a picture of a flower: do you like it?
4. <u>What's the weather like in your country</u> in November?

P.6-7
1. Chinese, Mandarin   2. Moroccan, Arabic   3. Italian, Italian   4. Malay, Malay
5. German, German   6. Greek, Greek   7. American, English
8. Kenyan, English   9. Japanese, Japanese   10. Brazilian, Portuguese